More Parts

P9-DFA-335

Tedd Arnold

PUFFIN BOOKS

To Mom and Dad—

There are still some things
I'd like explained.

PUFFIN BOOKS
Published by Penguin Group
Penguin Young Readers Group,
345 Hudson Street, New York, New York 10014, U.S.A.
Penguin Books Ltd, 80 Strand, London WC2R ORL, England
Penguin Books Australia Ltd, 250 Camberwell Road, Camberwell, Victoria 3124, Australia
Penguin Books Canada Ltd, 10 Alcorn Avenue, Toronto, Ontario, Canada M4V 3B2
Penguin Books (N.Z.) Ltd, 182-190 Wairau Road, Auckland 10, New Zealand

First published in the United States of America by Dial Books for Young Readers,
a division of Penguin Putnam Books for Young Readers, 2001
Published by Puffin Books, a division of Penguin Young Readers Group, 2003

34 36 38 40 39 37 35
Copyright © Tedd Arnold, 2001
All rights reserved

THE LIBRARY OF CONGRESS HAS CATALOGED THE DIAL EDITION AS FOLLOWS:
Arnold, Tedd.
More Parts / by Tedd Arnold
p. cm.
Summary: A young boy is worried about what will happen to his body
when he hears such expressions as "give him a hand" and "hold your tongue."
ISBN: 0-8037-1417-3 (hc)
[1. Body, Human—Fiction. 2. Figures of Speech—Fiction. 3. Stories in rhyme.]
I. Title.
PZ8.3.A647 Mm 2001 [E]—dc21 00-029050

Puffin Books ISBN 978-0-14-250149-8

Printed in the United States of America

Except in the United States of America, this book is sold subject to the condition that
it shall not, by way of trade or otherwise, be lent, re-sold, hired out, or otherwise
circulated without the publisher's prior consent in any form of binding or cover
other than that in which it is published and without a similar condition
including this condition being imposed on the subsequent purchaser.

Things are bad — and getting worse!
Each day it's something new.
With all the stuff I hear about
I don't know what to do.

One day I tripped on my red truck
And it just fell apart.
But when I told my mom, she said,
"I'll bet that broke your heart."

I guess that's possible. Who knows?
I don't think Mom would lie.
I'd better play more carefully.
This pillow's worth a try.

People say all kinds of things
That I don't understand.
Like when my dad asked me if I
Would please give him a hand.

I didn't know my hands come off,
And I don't want them to!
So I'll make sure that they stay on
With gloves and lots of glue.

Our next-door neighbor had a joke
He wanted us to hear.
He said, "It's sure to crack you up!"
I ran away in fear.

Who wants to hear a joke like that?
Not my idea of fun!
I gotta keep my head together.
It's my only one.

My teacher has me worried too.
This happened yesterday:
She said to stretch our arms and legs
Before we go and play.

I'm sure she thinks it's good for us,
But that's just too bizarre!
My arms and legs are long enough.
I like the way they are.

I know I've got a lot to learn.
I'm little and I'm young.
But what did Grandma really mean
When she said, "Hold your tongue"?

My tongue's a *slimy*, jiggly, squishy,
Slippery little squirt.
It'd be my luck to squeeze too hard
And lose it in the dirt.

So I decided that it's best
To stay here in my room.
'Cause who knows when some little thing
Just might lead to my

DOOM?

Then Mom and Dad came in and asked me,
"Why are you upset?"

I told them all the things I've heard
That get me in a sweat.

Like Coach, who says before each game
Is ready to begin,
He gets so nervous that he nearly
Jumps out of his skin.

Or what a friend said recently—
It gave me such a fright!
He claimed his baby sister screams
Her lungs out every night.

My skin could slip, my head may crack,
And I might break my heart.
I could lose my lungs, my hands—
Who knows when it might *start*?
What if quite by accident
My body flies apart?

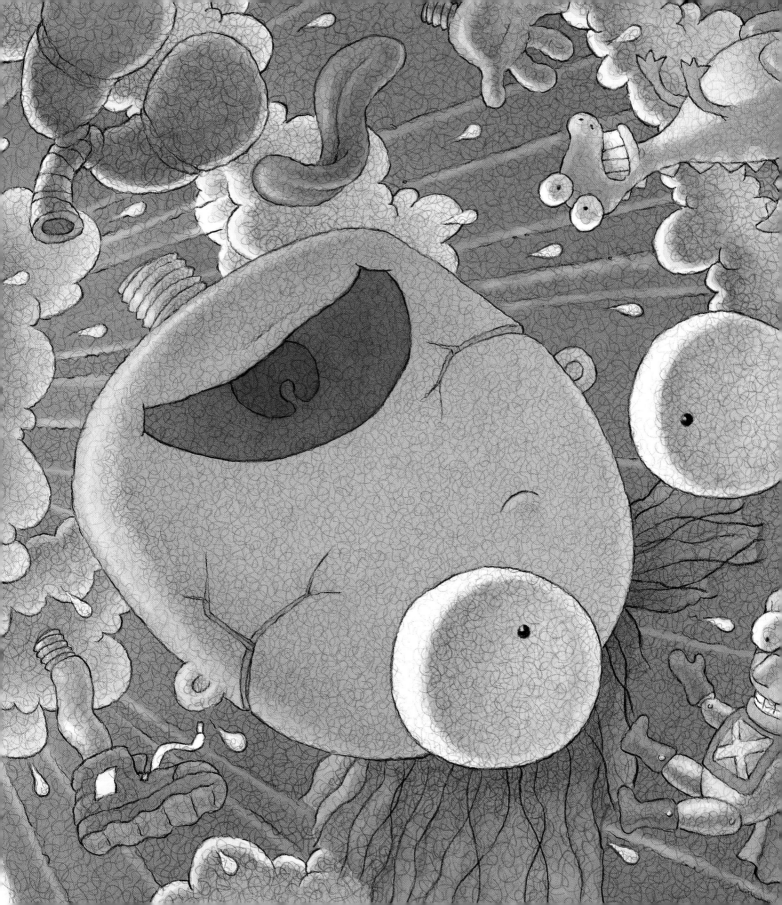

Mom and Dad just smiled and looked
Relieved that I'm okay.
And Mom explained to me about
The things that people say.

And though Dad laughed, I know he didn't
Mean to be unkind
When he said, "For a minute, son . . .